Oo-Ma-Ha Ta-Wa-Tha and Other Stories

Oo-Ma-Ha Ta-Wa-Tha and Other Stories

Susette La Flesche and Fannie Reed Griffin

MINT EDITIONS

Oo-Ma-Ha Ta-Wa-Tha and Other Stories was first published in 1898.

This edition published by Mint Editions 2021.

ISBN 9781513283364 | E-ISBN 9781513288383

Published by Mint Editions®

 MINT
EDITIONS

minteditionbooks.com

Publishing Director: Jennifer Newens
Design & Production: Rachel Lopez Metzger
Project Manager: Micaela Clark
Typesetting: Westchester Publishing Services

"The translations of the stories are as literal as possible. To get an Indian to relate a tribe legend to a white man is not a small undertaking. Their legends are sacred matters with them."

Through the kindness of Mr. Julius Meyer of Omaha, who has the largest and finest Indian relic collection in the west, and also of Henry Fontenelle and Louis Neil—two Omaha Indians—we obtained several photographs of chiefs which otherwise could not have been procured.

Contents

PREFACE

In remembrance of the Omahas, the tribe of Indians after which Omaha city is named, and who, less than fifty years ago, held an uncontested title to the land where Omaha city and the great Trans-Mississippi Exposition is located, this book is dedicated, that the memory of the tribe, its chieftains, its warriors and its maidens might be preserved. The book is edited by one who was herself born on Nebraska soil, and at whose father's house the chiefs of several Nebraska tribes were always received with a welcome, and given hospitable entertainment.

Most of the illustrations are the productions and reproductions of the brush and pencil of the daughter of E-sta-mah-za (Iron Eye), noted chief of the Omahas, pronounced by the tribe, Oo-mah-ha. The book also contains a copy of the treaty with the Omahas by which instrument the title of the land upon which Omaha city and the Trans-Mississippi Exposition is located passed to the United States government in 1854. Reproductions of the photographs of all, except one, of the chiefs (Tah-wah-gah-ha, or Village Maker, feared the camera, therefore his picture was never taken) who signed the treaty, with a short character sketch of each. The illustrations by Inshta Theumba (Bright Eyes) are believed to be the first artistic work by an American Indian ever published; and the book will be entertaining on that account alone. It is hoped that a souvenir of this kind will not only recall the wonderful progress made by the white people who have found homes in the valley of the Mississippi, but create and forever perpetuate a kindly feeling for the remnant of the Indian people still remaining, and who are slowly struggling upward toward a higher civilization.

Treaty with the Indians

March, 16, 1854.

Franklin Pierce, President of the United States of America, to all and singular to whom these presents shall come, Greeting:

Whereas a Treaty was made and concluded at the City of Washington, on the sixteenth day of March, one thousand eight hundred and fifty-four, by George W. Manypenny, Commissioner on the part of the United States, and the Omaha tribe of Indians, which treaty is in the words following, to wit:

Articles of agreement and convention made and concluded at the City of Washington this sixteenth day of March, one thousand eight hundred and fifty-four, by George W. Manypenny, as Commissioner on the part of the United States, and the following named chiefs of the Omaha tribe of Indians, viz: Shon-ga-ska, or Logan Fontenelle; E-sta-mah-za, or Joseph Le Flesche; Gra-tah-nah-je, or Standing Hawk; Gah-he-ga-gin-gah, or Little Chief; Tah-wah-gah-ha, or Village Maker; Wah-no-ke-ga, or Noise; So-da-nah-ze, or Yellow Smoke; they being thereto duly authorized by said tribe.

Article 1. The Omaha Indians cede to the United States all their lands west of the Missouri river, and south of a line drawn due west from a point in the center of the main channel of said Missouri river due east of where the Ayoway river disembogues out of the bluffs, to the western boundary of the Omaha country, and forever relinquish all right and title to the country south of said line. *Provided, however,* that if the country north of the said due west line, which is reserved by the Omahas for their future home, should not on exploration prove to be a satisfactory and suitable location for said Indians, the President may, with the consent of said Indians, set apart and assign to them, within or outside of the ceded country, a residence suited for and acceptable to them. And for the purpose of determining at once and definitely, it is agreed that a delegation of said Indians, in company with their agent, shall, immediately after the ratification of this instrument, proceed to examine the country hereby reserved, and if it please the delegation, and the Indians in counsel express themselves satisfied, then it shall be deemed and taken for their future home; but if otherwise, on the fact being reported to the President, he is authorized to cause a new location, of suitable extent, to be made for the future home of said Indians, and which shall not be more in extent than three hundred thousand acres, and then in that case, all the country belonging to the said Indians north of a said due west line, shall be and is hereby ceded to the United States by the said Indians, they to receive the same rate per acre for it, less the number of acres assigned in lieu of it for a home, as now paid for the land south of said line.

ARTICLE 2. The Omahas agree, that so soon after the United States shall make the necessary provision for fulfilling the stipulations of this instrument, as they can conveniently arrange their affairs, and not to exceed one year from its ratification, they will vacate the ceded country, and remove to the lands reserved herein by them, or to the other lands provided for in lieu thereof, in the preceding article, as the case may be.

ARTICLE 3. The Omahas relinquish to the United States all claims, for money or other thing, under former treaties, and likewise all claim which they may have heretofore, at any time, set up, to any land on the east side of the Missouri river: *Provided,* The Omahas shall still be entitled to and receive from the Government, the unpaid balance of the twenty-five thousand dollars appropriated for their use, by the act of thirtieth of August, 1851.

ARTICLE 4. In consideration of and payment for the country herein ceded, and the relinquishments herein made, the United States agree to pay to the Omaha Indians the several sums of money following, to wit:

1st. Forty thousand dollars per annum, for the term of three years, commencing on the first day of January, eighteen hundred and fifty-five.

2nd. Thirty thousand dollars per annum, for the term of ten years, next succeeding the three years.

3rd. Twenty thousand dollars per annum, for the term of fifteen years, next succeeding the ten years.

4th. Ten thousand dollars per annum, for the term of twelve years, next succeeding the fifteen years.

All which several sums of money shall be paid to the Omahas, or expended for their use and benefit, under the direction of the President of the United States, who may from time to time determine, at his discretion, what proportion of the annual payments, in this article provided for, if any, shall be paid to them in money, and what proportion shall be applied to and expended for their moral improvement and education; for such beneficial objects as in his judgment will be calculated to advance them in civilization; for buildings, opening farms, fencing, breaking land, providing stock, agricultural implements, seeds, etc.; for clothing, provisions, and merchandise; for iron, steel, arms and ammunition; for mechanics, and tools; and for medical purposes.

ARTICLE 5. In order to enable the said Indians to settle their affairs and to remove and subsist themselves for one year at their new home, and which they agree to do without further expense to the United States, and also to pay the expenses of the delegation who may be appointed to make the exploration provided for in article first, and to fence and break up two hundred acres of land at their new home, they shall receive from the United States, the further sum of forty-one thousand dollars, to be paid out and expended under the directions of the President, and in such manner as he shall approve.

ARTICLE 6. The President may, from time to time, at his discretion, cause the whole or such portion of the land hereby reserved, as he may think proper, or of such other land as may be selected in lieu thereof, as provided for in article first, to be surveyed into lots, and to assign to such Indian or Indians of said tribe as are willing to avail of the privilege, and who will locate on the same as a permanent home, if a single person over twenty-one years of age, one eighth of a section; to each family of two, one quarter section; to each family of three and not exceeding five, one-half section; to each family of six and not exceeding ten, one section; and to each family over ten in number, one-quarter section for every additional five members. And he may prescribe such rules and regulations as will insure to the family, in case of death of the head thereof, the possession and enjoyment of such permanent home and the improvements thereon. And the President may, at any time, in his discretion, after such person or family has made a location on the land assigned for a permanent home, issue a patent to such person or family for such assigned land, conditioned that the tract shall not be aliened or leased for a longer term than two years; and shall be exempt from levy, sale, or forfeiture, which conditions shall continue in force, until a State constitution, embracing such lands within its boundaries, shall have been formed, and the legislature of the state shall remove the restrictions. And if any such person or family shall at any time neglect or refuse to occupy and till a portion of the lands assigned, and on which they have located, or shall rove from place to place, the President may, if the patent shall have been issued, cancel the assignment, and may also withhold from such person or family, their proportion of the annuities or other moneys due them, until they shall have returned to such permanent home, and resumed the pursuits of industry; and in default of their return the tract may be declared abandoned, and thereafter assigned to some other person or family of such tribe, or disposed of as provided for the disposition of the excess of said land. And the residue of the land hereby reserved, or of that which may be selected in lieu thereof, after all of the Indian persons or families shall have had assigned to them permanent homes, may be sold for their benefit, under such laws, rules or regulations, as may hereafter be prescribed by the Congress or President of the United States. No State legislature shall remove the restrictions herein provided for, without the consent of Congress.

ARTICLE 7. Should the Omahas determine to make their permanent home north of the due west line named in the first article, the United States agree to protect them from the Sioux and all other hostile tribes, as long as the President may deem such protection necessary; and if other lands be assigned them, the same protection is guaranteed.

ARTICLE 8. The United States agree to erect for the Omahas at their new home, a grist and saw mill, and keep the same in repair, and provide a miller for ten years; also to erect a good blacksmith shop, supply the same with tools, and keep it in repair for ten years; and provide a good blacksmith for a like period; and to employ an experienced farmer for the term of ten years, to instruct the Indians in agriculture.

ARTICLE 9. The annuities of the Indians shall not be taken to pay the debts of individuals.

ARTICLE 10. The Omahas acknowledge their dependence on the government of the United States, and promise to be friendly with all the citizens thereof, and pledge themselves to commit no depredations on the property of such citizens. And should any one or more of them violate this pledge, and the fact be satisfactorily proven before the agent, the property taken shall be returned, or in default thereof, or if injured or destroyed, compensation may be made by the government out of their annuities. Nor will they make war on any other tribe, except in self-defense, but will submit all matters of difference between them and other Indians to the government of the United States, or its agent, for decision, and abide thereby. And if any of the said Omahas commit any depredations on any other Indians, the same rule shall prevail as that prescribed in this article in case of depredations against citizens.

ARTICLE 11. The Omahas acknowledge themselves indebted to Lewis Saunsoci, a half-breed, for services, the sum of one thousand dollars, which debt they have not been able to pay, and the United States agree to pay the same.

ARTICLE 12. The Omahas are desirous to exclude from their country the use of ardent spirits, and to prevent their people from drinking the same, and therefore it is provided that any Omaha who is guilty of bringing liquor into their country, or who drinks liquor, may have his or her proportion of the annuities withheld from him or her for such time as the President may determine.

ARTICLE 13. The board of foreign missions of the Presbyterian church have on the lands of the Omahas a manual labor boarding school, for the education of the Omaha, Otoe, and other Indian youth, which is now in successful operation, and as it will be some time before the necessary buildings can be erected on the reservation, and (it is) desirable that the school should not be suspended, it is agreed that the said board shall have four adjoining quarter sections of land, so as to include as near as may be all the improvements heretofore made by them, and the President is authorized to issue to the proper authority of said board, a patent in fee simple for such quarter sections.

ARTICLE 14. The Omahas agree that all the necessary roads, highways and railroads, which may be constructed as the country improves, and the lines of which may run through such tract as may be reserved for their permanent home, shall have a right of way through the reservation, a just compensation being paid therefor in money.

ARTICLE 15. This treaty shall be obligatory on the contracting parties as soon as the same shall be ratified by the President and Senate of the United States.

In testimony whereof, the said George W. Manypenny, commissioner as aforesaid, and the undersigned chiefs, of the Omaha tribe of Indians, have hereunto set their hands and seals, at the place and on the day and year hereinbefore written.

GEORGE W. MANYPENNY,
Commissioner.

(L. S.)

Shon-ga-ska, or Logan Fontenelle,
    his x mark.   (L. S.)
E-sta-mah-za, or Joseph LeFlesche,
    his x mark.   (L. S.)

Gra-tah-nah-je, or Standing Hawk,
> his x mark. (L. S.)

Gah-he-ga-gin-gah, or Little Chief,
> his x mark. (L. S.)

Tah-wah-gah-ha, or Village Maker,
> his x mark. (L. S.)

Wah-no-ke-ga, or Noise,
> his x mark. (L. S.)

So-da-nah-ze, or Yellow Smoke,
> his x mark. (L. S.)

Executed in the presence of us:

James M. Gatewood, Indian Agent.
James Goszler.
Charles Calvert.
James D. Kerr.
Henry Beard.
Alfred Chapman.
Louis Saunsoci, Interpreter.

And whereas the said Treaty having been submitted to the Senate of the United States for its constitutional action thereon, the Senate did, on the seventeenth day of April, one thousand eight hundred and fifty-four, amend the same by a resolution in the words and figures following, to-wit:

> In Executive Session,
> Senate of the United States,
> April 17th, 1854

Resolved, (two-thirds of the senators present concurring), That the Senate advise and consent to the ratification of the articles of agreement and convention made and concluded at the City of Washington this (the) sixteenth day of March, one thousand eight hundred and fifty-four, by George W. Manypenny as Commissioner on the part of the United States, and the following named chiefs of the Omaha tribe of Indians, viz: Shon-ga-ska, or Logan Fontenelle; E-sta-mah-za, or Joseph La Flesche; Gra-tah-nah-je, or Standing Hawk; Gah-he-ga-gin-gah, or Little Chief; Tah-wah-gah-ha, or Village Maker; Wah-no-ke-ga, or Noise; So-da-nah-ze, or Yellow Smoke, they being thereto duly authorized by said tribe; with the following amendment,—Article 3, line 3, strike out "1851" and insert 1852.

Attest:

ASBURY DICKENS, Secretary

Now, therefore, be it known, that I, FRANKLIN PIERCE, President of the United States of America, do, in pursuance of the advice and consent of the Senate, as expressed in their resolution of the seventeenth day of April, one thousand eight hundred and fifty-four, accept, ratify, and confirm the said treaty as amended.

In testimony whereof, I have caused the seal of the United States to be hereunto affixed, having signed the same with my hand.

(L. S.) Done at the City of Washington, this twenty-first day of June, in the year of our Lord one thousand eight hundred and fifty-four, and of the Independence of the United States the seventy-eighth.

FRANKLIN PIERCE

By the President:
W. L. MARCY, Secretary of State

Shon-ga-ska, or Logan Fontenelle

O f the chiefs who signed the treaty conveying the title of the land to the United States, where Omaha and the Trans-Mississippi Exposition now stand, the first was Logan Fontenelle. He was the only one among them who could read, write or speak English. He was elected chief for the express purpose of helping the Indians to make the treaty with the United States.

Mr. Fontenelle was tall, of courtly bearing, pleasing manners, and universally respected by the white people as well as by the Indians. He was a great personal friend of Iron Eye (Joseph La Flesche), and was a well educated man, being one-half French.

He accompanied the chiefs to Washington, and although he had formerly acted as their interpreter, on this occasion another interpreter was taken, and Shon-ga-ska made his speeches to the President and Commissioner in the Omaha language; and they were interpreted into English by Louis Saunsoci, who was official interpreter upon this visit.

After his return from Washington, and the Omahas were ordered to move to their new reservation, where they still reside, about seventy miles north of Omaha on the Missouri river. Fontenelle is said to have made a vigorous protest against the removal, until the government fulfilled its part of the agreement.

The treaty provided that the government of the United States would protect the Omahas against the Sioux, who were at that time roaming all over the northern part of Nebraska, and were the old enemies of the Omahas.

When the Indians were ordered to go to the reservation, no provisions were made for their protection, and Fontenelle is said to have made a speech at Bellevue, before they started. Some fragments of this speech have been preserved by the State Historical Society.

He declared it was murder, and nothing but murder, to place the unarmed and defenseless Omahas right in the path of their hereditary enemies. He finally placed his hand on his revolver and said, "This is good for six Sioux. We will go and meet our fate."

It was but a short time after, when on a hunt (for the Omahas were forced to hunt or starve), that an overwhelming number of the Sioux made onslaught on the Omaha hunting party. Logan Fontenelle fought as long as he could raise his hand. He did not quite make his assertion good, but three dead Sioux were found near his body.

Some days after the fight, his body was recovered and brought back to the camp of the Omahas. The whole tribe went into mourning. Strange stories are told in the tents of the Omahas today about the ceremonies that were performed by the club or secret society, among the Indians, to which he belonged.

Col. Sarpy sent to St. Joseph, Missouri, and hired a Protestant Episcopal minister to come to Bellevue and read the Episcopal services over the remains. The white people in all that region of the country, being mostly French traders, assembled the day that he was buried.

Logan Fontenelle's name, among all classes of the Omahas, is to this day held in great reverence.

E-sta-mah-za, or Joseph La Flesche

I ron Eye, the second signer of the treaty, is known to the whites as Joseph La Flesche. He was a man of very great natural ability. He had no education, could not read, write, or speak English, but he always impressed one as a man of thought and good judgment. He was an unlearned, natural philosopher. How he obtained his vast store of knowledge, when he could not read, and had no association with men of learning, was always a mystery. When the great Indian habeas corpus case was first stated to him, he instantly replied with a clear statement of the fundamental and underlying principles upon which the case should be fought in the courts. When his views were submitted to the attorneys, Messrs. Poppleton and Webster, they immediately admitted their force and soundness, and acted upon them.

Early in life the abilities of Iron Eye were recognized by the wise and statesman-like old head chief, Big Elk, who foresaw the changes that were coming, and desired a wise and prudent ruler to follow him. Big Elk had a son who, according to Indian custom, would inherit the head chieftainship, but he was a child, and had a weak physical constitution. The old chief knew that the great transformation which was bound to overthrow the customs of Indian life, would come before his boy would arrive at mature years, and he resolved that Iron Eye should take the head chieftainship and pilot the tribe through that dangerous period.

Big Elk took every precaution to impress upon the tribe that Iron Eye should inherit from him the full authority which he himself enjoyed, and was very careful to observe all the forms and ceremonies which the customs of the tribe required in such cases. He therefore sent by the officer, whose duty it was to carry it, the tobacco bag to Iron Eye, who received it with all the formalities prescribed on such occasions.

Then Big Elk "pipe danced" Iron Eye's wife (this occurred two years after her marriage). By this ceremony, Big Elk adopted Iron Eye as his son, and announced by the public crier that he had done so. Then in public, in the presence of Iron Eye, Big Elk further declared, so that there could be no possibility of misunderstanding, that Iron Eye was his "oldest" son and that he wished Iron Eye to inherit the chieftainship from him.

After that he caused Iron Eye to give four ceremonial feasts, which the Indian customs required when one was declared the inheritor of the chieftainship.

At these feasts all the chiefs and all the members of the tribe assented, for they all loved Iron Eye for his generosity and kindness to the tribe, respected his ability and feared his power. Four times these ceremonies were repeated,* and ever after during Big Elk's life, on all proper occasions, Iron Eye was recognized as their chief.

Several years later the Indians were having a feast. One afternoon Big Elk went out hunting and killed a deer with a tomahawk. A few hours later he was stricken with a fever then epidemic among the Indians. Big Elk called for Iron Eye, and said: "My son, give me some medicine." An Indian runner was sent to Bellevue for medicine, but it was a three days' journey, and when the carrier returned it was too late. Just before the old chief died he sent for Iron Eye, and said: "My son, I give you all my papers from Washington, and I make you head chief. You will occupy my place. When your brother is of age (meaning his own young son) you can do for him as is best. I leave him in your charge."

When dying, seeing Louis, the young son of Iron Eye, he raised his hand, and said: "My grandchild—" attempted to speak further, but could not.

Iron Eye then assumed the chieftainship of the tribe, all the chiefs consenting. The action of the tribe was approved by the commissioner of Indian affairs, Manypenny, and other authorities at Washington. Iron Eye's papers were sent to him, bearing the great seal from Washington. They are now in possession of his son, Frank La Flesche, who is employed in the Indian Department at Washington, D. C.

It was impossible that a man of Iron Eye's character, determined as he was that the tribe should be brought as soon as possible to abandon the Indian mode of life, go to farming and send their children to school, should not meet with fierce opposition among his own people. It did, and the result was, that the tribe was divided into two parties. The one called the "Chief's party", being opposed to the education of their children and to farming, and the other called the "Young Men's party," who favored education, desired to adopt the customs of the whites, and go to farming.

---

* Everything has to be repeated four times in an Indian tribe before it has validity.

Of the latter party Iron Eye was the head, and a political warfare of the greatest bitterness was waged. Iron Eye found that he had not only half of the tribe arrayed against him, but often the agent, the agent's employes and the authorities at Washington. It was not to the interest of this class of white men that the Indians should become intelligent, self-supporting farmers.

Iron Eye employed every means he could command in the contest. He did not believe in Indian superstitions; but he used them to aid him in this dispute, for he thoroughly believed that upon the success of the principles he advocated depended the future existence of his people. He often said to them: "It is either civilization or extermination."

Father Hamilton related a story of the way Iron Eye would appeal to their superstitions. On returning from a trip to Washington, Iron Eye brought home with him a small electric battery and a patent cork leg (for some years before he had lost a leg, and always walked around on an old-fashioned substitute).

He made a feast, and invited all the chiefs and head men of the tribe. When they were assembled, and had eaten, he made them a speech something after this fashion:

"You all believe in the power of your medicine men. However much power they may have, it is nothing compared with that of the whites. Your medicine is but as a breath that vanishes, when compared with theirs. You cannot resist them; it is useless to try. Now I will show you something of the power of the white man's medicine."

He then had the chiefs join hands and take hold of the handles of the battery. Then suddenly he turned it on full force, and stood gravely to one side and watched their contortions. He finally turned the battery off, and while the chiefs were trying to recover their dignity, he stepped aside, and came walking in, to all appearance having in a minute or two grown a new leg.

The astonishment of the chiefs and medicine men were beyond description. Iron Eye sat down on a box, crossed his legs, moved his wooden foot up and down, then got up and walked around. By this time the chiefs and medicine men were so frightened that they were about to flee from his presence.

He commanded them all to be seated. Everyone immediately obeyed. There was a power in that white man's medicine of which they were all afraid. Then he made a long speech to them, showed them his wooden leg, explained the working of the electric battery, and told them there was no such thing as "big medicine," either among the Indians or the whites, and impressed upon them the fact that the whites were not great and powerful because of any magic power, but because they all worked and sent their children to school.

While one or two were converted, the result of the performance was that the opposition chiefs and medicine men hated him worse than ever.

During these years there was a furor in all the Indian tribes. The Otoe Indians sent a delegation to the Omaha tribe to aid those Indians who were opposed to civilization. Iron Eye had a brother who was a chief in the Ponca tribe, and he was anxious that they, too, should advance. In May, 1876, he dictated the following letter, and sent it to his brother, White Swan. It will give an idea of the way he tried to instruct the Indians. The letter read as follows:

OMAHA AGENCY, May, 1876

DEAR BROTHER

"I have some news to send you, but it is not good news. The Otoes came up here to visit us. Instantly, upon their arrival, the whole tribe got together and had a council. I did not hear all that was done, but I know that it is the same thing that I have been hearing for the last ten years. The Otoes told them that all the Indians where they came from, sent word to the Omahas that trying to be like the white people was very bad; that all who had tried to do it were badly off, but that those who had staid in the Indian customs were doing well. They had been sent to say that all who attempted to do like the white people, had given it up, and should go back to their old ways. It was too hard.

"The chief's party believed what they said, and they are more determined than ever to resist any step toward advancement. I think, however, that all of the Young men's party turned their backs on them.

"There are some good things by which we live.

"First—The God above made this world and gave it to us to live in.

"Second—The white men have been sent to teach us how to live.

"Third—God has made the earth to yield her fruit to us.

"Fourth—God has given us hands with which we can work.

"Look back on the lives of your fathers and grandfathers; then look at yourselves, and see how far you have gone ahead, and seeing this, do not stop and turn back to them, but go forward. Look ahead and you will see nothing but the white man. The future is full of the white man, and we shall be as nothing before them.

"Do not think that if anyone cheats you or does you wrong, that you will do the same to him. Look out for yourselves. Take care of yourselves."

From your brother,
Joseph La Flesche

Iron Eye always gave the missionaries among the Omahas his sympathy and earnest support. He was among the first to unite with the church after Father Hamilton came to the tribe, and was the life-long friend of this patient man of God.

The next Sunday after Iron Eye united with the church, the room in which public services were held would not hold one-fifth of the Indians that attended. For several Sundays the same Indians were always there. This constant church-going on the part of the Indians, many of whom had never before been seen at the church services, was a mystery to Father Hamilton. It was winter, and some of the days on which they came were exceedingly cold and stormy. But that made no difference; when Sunday came, the Indians assembled—men, women and children, dogs and ponies, by the hundreds.

Finally Father Hamilton asked Iron Eye what made the Indians all at once take a notion to go to church in such large numbers.

Said Iron Eye, "It is good for the Indians to go to church. I want them to learn to be Christians, so I ordered them to go."

Father Hamilton undertook to explain to him that the Christian religion could not be propagated in that way. But Iron Eye would not agree, and said:

"This new way that you teach us is good. You have read to me the words of the Son of God, from the book God gave to you, and the words were good. The words of that book are not like what the old men have taught us. What they have taught us is foolishness. When you read God's book to the Indians, and explain to them what it means, it teaches them to walk in the right way. Therefore, I ordered them to go every Sunday and hear you read from God's book, and listen to you while you explain it."

A long argument followed, and the subject was discussed several hours a day for three days. At last Iron Eye said that Father Hamilton must take God's book, read it all through, and then tell him what the book said about it.

Father Hamilton hunted up a great many scriptural texts which he thought bore upon the question, but none of them convinced Iron Eye, until he read to him the following:

"My kingdom is not of this world; if my kingdom were of this world, then would my servants fight."

Iron Eye sat still in deep thought for a long time. At last he arose, and said he must think over the subject more, and went away.

When Iron Eye returned two or three days afterwards, he seemed to be a changed man. His manner, always fascinating and attractive, was now more kindly than ever.

"My friend," he said, "you have often read to me out of God's book, and I thought that I understood the meaning of it, but I did not. Now it seems to me that that book tells us about two things instead of one thing. It tells us how to do, that we may get things to eat and drink, so that we may live here on the earth that God gave us. That refers only to the body. About such things as that, if I know a better way I may give orders. But there is a something, different from this. It does not pertain to the body—what we shall eat, drink or wear—but to the heart and soul. I cannot make a man good by issuing an order. I can say to a man, 'You build a house and live in it, and no longer live in a tent.' He will go and do it. But I cannot say to a man, 'Your heart is bad, have a good heart hereafter.' There is a something over which no man, however great his authority—even if it is as great as that of the Great Father at Washington—can have control. Over that God alone can rule."

The next Sunday, Iron Eye made an address to the Indians. Father Hamilton said, that at no Synod or General Assembly did he ever here a more profound and philosophical discourse on the invisible kingdom of God. The order was revoked, and from that time on the little Indian church built up its membership from those who, of their own free will, chose to attend.

As soon as the Indians obtained titles to lands in severalty, Iron Eye selected a location out on the Logan river, near the town of Bancroft, Nebraska. He built a good two-story house and barn, bought a supply of the latest improved farm machinery, and opened up a large farm.

There were many sides to Iron Eye's character. He was a great hunter, and, in defense of his tribe, he was a fierce warrior. Many a Sioux, in the series of battles between them and the Omahas, started on his long journey to the happy hunting ground through the unerring aim of his bow or rifle. He was a trader, and at one time had accumulated a large fortune, several thousand dollars of which he loaned a white man, who refused to pay, and then Iron Eye felt the full force of the old Indian system, when he learned that an Indian could not sue or be sued in the white man's courts of law. So his creditor could not be made to pay, and Iron Eye lost all his money.

Still another side of his character is illustrated by an incident related by his daughter, Inshta Theumba.

"We were out on the buffalo hunt. I was a little bit of a thing when it happened, long before I could speak English, but the impression it made on me seems to grow stronger as I grow older. Father could neither read, write or speak English; and this little insight into his character shows plainly that moral worth of the very highest can exist, aside from all white civilization and education.

"It was evening; the tents had been pitched for the night, the camp-fire had been made, and mother and the other women were cooking supper over it. It was a soft, yellow sunset, with scarcely any wind. I was playing near my father, when a little Indian boy, a playmate, came up and gave me a little bird he had found. I was very much pleased, and showed it to father and mother, and tried to feed it and make it drink. After I had amused myself with it for a time, my father said to me, 'My daughter, bring your bird to me.' When I took it to him, he held it in his hand a moment, smoothed its feathers gently, and then said, 'Daughter, I will tell you what you might do with it. Take it carefully in your hand, out yonder where there are no tents, where the high grass is, put it softly down on the ground, and say as you put it down: God, I give you back your little bird. Have pity on me, as I have pity on your bird.'

"I said, 'Does it belong to God?' He said, 'Yes, and he will be pleased if you do not hurt it, but give it back to him to take care of.' I was very much impressed, and carefully followed out his directions, saying over the little prayer he had told me to say.

"Whenever I think of my father in connection with this incident, Tennyson's lines come into my mind:

"'He prayeth best, who loveth best,
All things both great and small,
For the dear God who loveth us,
He made and loveth all.'"

After a hard day's labor he took a severe cold, and died very suddenly, September 23, 1888.

The white people came from miles around to attend his funeral. It is said to have been the largest funeral procession ever seen in that part of the state. He is buried in the cemetery just south of Bancroft, where a modest marble shaft marks the last resting-place of this most remarkable man.

Gra-tah-nah-je, or Standing Hawk

S tanding Hawk was one of the hereditary chiefs of the Omaha tribe. He lived for many years after the treaty was made, near the Omaha Mission, in a two-story frame house, which had been built by Iron Eye, in the early years of his residence there, and used partly for a trading post. Standing Hawk was a thorough Indian, and believed in all the Indian superstitions, and practiced them until the day of his death. He was a man of good character; and farmed so far as he was able to do so. But to change from the Indian mode of living to that of civilization came to him too late in life.

He believed in owning lands in severalty, and often said that while he was too old to learn the white people's ways, his children should learn them.

Gah-he-ga-gin-gah, or Little Chief

Little Chief died shortly after the treaty was made. He was a man highly respected by all who knew him. He made one variation from the Indian customs. He treated his wife as if she were a queen. He never allowed her to work more than was absolutely necessary. She was a woman of the highest character.

This marked difference of Little Chief's treatment of his wife to that of the other Indians is still remembered in the tribe.

His wife is still living, and preserves all the dignity of her former years. Among the Indian customs to which she adheres, is the practice of making a formal visit once a year, to all the members of the tribe who (under the old Indian customs) were of equal rank with herself. She is always treated with the greatest consideration by all members of the tribe.

At Little Chief's funeral a large concourse of people, including missionaries, agents and employes, assembled. The Indian burial ceremonies were observed in full, for the last time, in the Omaha tribe. His horse, led to the grave, covered with blankets and other personal belongings of the chief, was strangled; also his favorite dog was killed, that they might accompany him on his long journey to the happy hunting grounds.

Tah-wah-gah-ha, or Village Maker

Village Maker was a very old man at the time the treaty was made, and died a short time afterwards.

But few traditions concerning him are preserved by the Indians. Among them is one which declares that Village Maker was a great hunter, always providing plenty for his family and the entertainment of visiting chiefs. It is said that he was a good man, and that very early in life he told the Indians that the white people would finally fill all the land, and that the Indians must turn from hunting to farming. His descendants are quite numerous in the tribe today; and they always speak with the greatest reverence of old Village Maker.

Wah-no-ke-ga, or Noise

Noise was one of the signers of the treaty, but like Village Maker, he was an old man at that time, and died soon afterwards. But little is known about him, as his band was not as numerous as some others in the tribe.

He had met but a few white people, or "the big knives," as they were called at that time by the Omahas. The first people with whom they came in familiar contact were the French traders. The Indians called them white natives, in contra-distinction from all other white foreigners.

Noise was a thorough believer in all the Indian customs, and lived in accordance with them until his death.

So-da-nah-ze, or Yellow Smoke

Yellow Smoke, the last signer of the treaty, lived to a good old age. He was one of the first Indians who made a profession of the Christian religion, and for years was an elder in the Presbyterian church, established by Father Hamilton.

Yellow Smoke was what would be called, among the white people, "a pillar of the church." He never failed to be present at any public service, and every prayer meeting, when it was at all possible for him to do so.

When he was in Washington, some one made him a present of a silk hat. Yellow Smoke preserved this to the day of his death, and always, when attending church, when the weather was fair, would wear that hat. He had another silk hat that he wore on other occasions, but this one he always kept for church.

To see Yellow Smoke walk into church with his silk hat and blanket on, to one who did not know him, would cause a smile, but if one waited until it came his turn to speak, he would always hear something well worth remembering.

An educated white man who often attended the church, said that he never heard, anywhere, finer religious addresses than he had heard delivered in that church by Yellow Smoke.

Being a thorough Christian, he abandoned all the Indian customs, and adopted those, as far as he could, of the whites. It may be said of him that he was a conscientious believer and follower of the Lowly Nazarene. He and Big Elk, who is a descendant of the old chief Big Elk, were, for years, the leaders of the Indian Presbyterian church on the reservation, and have had the confidence and respect of all the missionaries and ministers who knew them.

To the Driving Cloud

By H. W. Longfellow

Gloomy and dark art thou, O chief of the mighty Omawhaws;
Gloomy and dark as the driving cloud, whose name thou hast taken.
Wrapt in the scarlet blanket, I see thee stalk through the city's
Narrow and populous streets, as once by the margin of rivers,
Stalked those birds unknown, that have left us only their footprints.
What, in a few short years, will remain of thy race but the footprints?

How canst thou walk in these streets, who hast trod the green turf of
  the prairies?
How canst thou breathe in this air, who hast breathed the sweet air of
  the mountains?
Ah! 'Tis vain that with lordly looks of disdain thou dost challenge
Looks of dislike in return, and question these walls and these
  pavements,
Claiming the soil for thy hunting-grounds, while down-trodden
  millions
Starve in the garrets of Europe, and cry from its caverns that they,
  too,
Have been created heirs of the earth, and claim its division!
Back, then; back to thy woods in the regions west of the Wabash!
There, as a monarch thou reignest. In autumn the leaves of the maple
Pave the floors of thy palace-halls with gold, and in the summer
Pine trees waft through its chambers the odorous breath of their
  branches.
There thou art strong and great, a hero, a tamer of horses!
There thou chasest the stately stag on the banks of the Elkhorn,
Or by the roar of the Running Water, or where the Omawhaw
Calls thee, and leaps through the wild ravine like a brave of the
  Blackfeet!

Lo! the big thunder canoe, that steadily breasts the Missouri's
Merciless current! And yonder, afar on the prairies, the camp-fires
Gleam through the night; and the cloud of dust in the gray of the
  daybreak

Marks not the buffalo's track, nor the Mandan's dexterous horse race;
It is a caravan, whitening the desert where dwell the Comanches!
Ha! how the breath of these Saxons and Celts, like the blast of the
    east wind,
Drifts evermore to the west the scanty smokes of the wigwams!

Big Elk

After Black Bird,* who was given a national reputation, and very unfairly so, by Washington Irving, the next most noted chief in the history of the Omahas was Big Elk, of whom a great deal has been said in the biography of Iron Eye.

Big Elk, on the other hand, was noted for his kindness of heart and general good judgment, an instance of which may be found in another part of this souvenir, in the story of the French Captives.

Some twenty years ago, an old Omaha Indian told a white friend that the memory of Big Elk in his family would never die. He said that all the members of his father's family were poor, that they had never owned a horse, and when they were out on long buffalo hunts, they had to travel on foot and carry their baggage on their backs, and when returning, whatever robes, furs, or meat they procured, had to be carried in the same way.

One day his father, almost worn out from carrying a heavy pack, sat down by the way to rest, when Big Elk came by, and seeing the old man was nearly exhausted, he took pity on him and gave him his own horse. "That," said the old Omaha, "was the only horse my father ever owned. And he was no relation to Big Elk."

He succeeded Black Bird as head chief of the tribe, but he only lived a little past middle age, and died of an epidemic fever, prevalent at that time among the Omaha Indians. He died near the river, just below the bluff where Black Bird was buried.

He was buried on one of the hills south of where the Omaha agency building now stand.

So universally loved and respected was Big Elk by all the members of the Omaha tribe, that it is said that no member of that tribe has ever been heard to say anything other than that Big Elk was a great and good chief.

---

* The reputation of Black Bird in his tribe was, that he was a cruel and very unjust ruler of his people.

Wa-ja-pa's Letter

My Friend: As I am thinking of you today, I send you a letter of a few words. My friend, what I speak I hope you understand. The one thing that I wrote last winter to tell you about, last winter's words continue; but I shall tell you again. As to our being in this land, God put us here, and so we are here. Before the white people came hither, we thought it was our land. But when the Great Father* said the land was to be sold, it was sold, and a very small part remains to us of all that used to be ours. And now the white people wish to take that from us! They wish to send us to a far-off land. It is very hard for us. To take our land from us is very much like killing us.

"We wish to live, so I send you this letter. We tell you that we think of becoming citizens, because you (whites) have a bad opinion of the life and customs of Indians. Most truly do we tell you what is said. And when we become citizens we wish to keep our own land, therefore we wish to become citizens. I wish to tell you all this is hard for us. My friend, white people, Americans, those who have seen the Indians, and know them, when they tell you anything, they tell you straight truth. But those who have not seen us at all, say: 'Indians are bad.' Or when they have talked very little with us, they tell how very bad the Indians are.

"And, my friend, we hope that you all will open your hearts and think of God, and have pity on us Indians. For, by night and by day, we are in constant dread of some unseen evil.

"My friend, again another matter, in a very few words, I wish to speak about. It has been said: 'You are to have white soldiers reside among us.' But we know the soldiers, we know them, so we fear them. We do not want them, and all the Indians do not want the soldiers. From the days of the former Indians we have had them, so we know them. They act as if they were the only human beings. And whatever Indian woman they wish to dishonor, without taking her at all for a wife, they dishonor her, and they treat us just as if we were hogs and dogs. Therefore, we do not want them. The Indians are not the first to do what is bad. The soldiers first cover up their own bad deeds, and having covered up their own, they show to the Great Father the bad deeds of an Indian.

---

* The President. Referring to the white people generally, or the government.

"Although I shall repeat something, still I will say it again. The Indians called Sioux hate us Indians, who, having sold our lands to the Great Father, are now farming. You think that all the Indians are alike, but we are not alike. Some desire to be on the side of the white people, and some, who are called Sioux, are not so, and yet you think that we are exactly alike, when we are not so. We are not like them. We are all of different nations; you whites, too, are of different nations, and so are we. If the Sioux hate us, and if you, too, hate us, how can we live? We wish to live, we wish to go towards you. Even if we should fail, still we wish to get something for ourselves—that is, to become citizens. For only in that way can it be good for us.

"I have told you enough about that. And now I will tell you another thing. As we wish to live, we are working for ourselves. And we do so because we know very well that it will be good for us, and yet we have fared very hard this year. The heat was so great that our wheat was withered, and did not bring more than from thirty to forty cents a bushel. Therefore, we are just as if we had not made anything at all for ourselves; though we have corn, potatoes, and different kinds of vegetables.

"When we see these white-skin people, we think they are prospering, so we desire it (civilization). We know that all your agricultural implements, and other machines, are useful in getting one's living, and for the last three years we have had some tools.

"We have tried working, and know very well that it is good, so we desire it. As we write this letter to you, God is sitting with us, as it were; therefore, we hope that the white people will stop talking about our land (or against us).

"We wish to keep what is ours, so we petition you, and your people, too, who are helping us, we pray to you, and you who are on the other side, we pray to you also: Have pity on us Omaha Indians. We do not mean all the other tribes—ourselves alone, do we mean.

WA-JA-PA

A Dream Woman

It was over sixty years ago, when I was a little girl, that we camped near the Nishnabotna, at a place the Indians called Wa-a-hi-da O-thu-cump-pi (Beautiful in the Distance), opposite where Bellevue now stands. The place was thickly wooded, and in the beautiful grove the tents were set up.

"There were the tents of my brothers, Long Wing and Walking in the Rain; my uncle, Wi-thu-gun, as well as my father and mother, who had a tent of their own. The little girls with whom I dearly loved to play all day long, were Hin-na-gi (The Chief Woman), Gun-tha-i (The Wanted One) and Ha-sa-gii.

"One evening I cried for some deer marrow, and my uncle said, 'Do not cry any more, Hin-ua-sun,* tomorrow you shall have what you want.' Before the break of day, while we were still asleep, my uncle went away to look for deer.

"It was always a treat for us children, when the hunter brought home the venison, to have our mothers break the leg-bones of the deer and give us the marrow.

"After we had our breakfast, Hin-na-gi, Gun-tha-i and Ha-sa-gii came running from the tents, and said: 'Come on, Hin-ua-sun, bring your little pail, and we will go and look for wild beans, so we can cook them. Be sure and bring your knife, too, so we can make some dishes.'

"Holding my little short, red-handled knife in one hand, and my little pail in the other, I ran on into the woods with my companions.

"The great cottonwood trees that lay decaying on the ground were our especial delight, for out of their thick bark, which we pulled off, we made dishes, pails and tents, which we used in our play.

"We went to the larger logs which lay here and there, and putting in our hands we scraped out great handfuls of wild beans, which the little mice had stored away for their winter's living. After we had washed the wild beans clean and white, we put them in our little pail. Hin-na-gii planted a thick, round stick in the ground, and taking a stick with a notch in it, she tied it to the upright one, and then put the little pail on the notched stick, and our beans were ready to be cooked.

---

* Means a Relative.

"We built our fire and then sat down to make our bark dishes. We hollowed out the thick cottonwood bark and trimmed them into round shapes, like dishes of wood our mothers had. My dish was crooked, and I could not get it round like the other girls, which made me feel bad.

"'The beans are not boiling yet, so let us make a tent,' said Hin-na-gii, who was the oldest. 'We can go in and lie down while we are waiting for them.'

"We selected the tent-poles we wanted, and tying four together at the top, we set them on the ground so they would form a pyramid. We placed the rest of the poles in place, and then took great sheets of the cottonwood bark for our tent-cloth, and our bark house was ready.

"I put my little dish at my head, near my pillow of bark, and we all laid down. I went sound asleep, but the other girls did not go to sleep. They ate the beans, when they were done, and then, without waking me, they went home and left me alone in the tent.

"If I had dreamed it when I slept, I should have said it was a dream; but I awoke very suddenly, and looking around found the tent empty. Sleeping opposite the tent door, I raised my eyes, and there stood a most beautiful Indian woman, in a magnificent Indian dress. Looking at me, she gave me such a beautiful smile that I can never forget it. I turned around, and taking my little pail in one hand, and grasping my shawl in the other, I looked again towards the door, but the beautiful woman with the lovely smile had gone.

"As I ran home to the tents, I looked everywhere, but I saw nothing on the way. Raising the door-flap, I knelt down to enter the tent, where my uncle, who had the leg-bones of the deer ready for me, threw them toward me.

"'Uncle!' I said, and laughed in delight; but my uncle said, 'Sister, see; her mouth is crooked,' and mother said, 'My poor child.'

"Then we heard the voice of my brother from his tent, as he said, sternly:

"'It must be their work' (meaning ghosts). 'Treat your niece with the medicines that you know how to make, and do your best for her.'

"So my uncle went out, and brought in two roots, one of which he used as a wash, and the other I had to hold pieces of in my mouth all the time.

"Four is the magic number of the Indians, so for four days he treated me, and my mouth was straight again, although I do not remember the exact number of days this took.

"When my uncle went out to hunt, he examined the place where our bark tent stood, and there he found a great many very old graves of Indians, that had been buried many, many years before.

"They all said it was a ghost I saw, but I never thought so. My uncle, who was much gifted, was an interpreter of dreams, and this was the interpretation of my vision:

"'That women of all ranks or stations, and of all races, would smile on me.'

"I never used to tell this, because I thought it was a vision sent to me, and I was gifted to see visions, and so should not tell it, for it was the custom of my people, but since I have become a believer in the true God, and know there is nothing in the world beside Him, I have told this to show that I have put all such things away as not fitting a believer in the true Son of God."

LOUIS

My mother must be over seventy years of age, as near as we can make out, and yet to this day she cannot speak of my brother Louis' death without her eyes filling with tears. He was older than myself, and I am probably the only one of her children now living who can remember him. As young as I was at the time of his death, his individuality made such a strong impression on me, that I can, even now, at times, hear his merry laugh and shout, as he played with the other Indian boys at his games, and his sunny face, like a gleam of sunshine, flashes before my memory. My father had placed him at the Omaha Mission School, as he placed all of his children, one after the other, as they grew old enough to attend. His desire to have his children learn to speak English, and educate them as the white people were educated, was very strong.

"At the time of Louis' death, he was probably nine or ten years old. Father and mother had gone on a visit to the Pawnees, leaving him at the Mission. My grandmother had been left at home, at the Indian village, about three miles from the Mission. In the Mission building was a very large room in the third story which had been set aside as a bed-room for the little Indian boys who attended the school. One day, Kaghaumba, a family friend, went to visit the Mission. He heard from the other boys that Louis was sick, and going up into the bed-room, found little Louis in this great, bare room, without any attendance whatever, the teacher probably thinking that he was sick with some childish ailment. Kaghaumba, who could not speak a word of English, was so indignant that he wrapped the boy up in his blanket and carried him home to his grandmother, without informing the teacher. In two or three days Louis died, and father and mother were met by a runner, while still a day's journey from home, and told that their beautiful boy, whom they had left so full of life and vitality, was dead. On reaching home, mother says that father lay all night with his dead boy in his arms; that he was a changed man from that time, and never seemed the same as he was before.

"The most vivid impression that remains in my memory of that sad time is, that during one of the intervals when there was stillness and quiet, because the wailing of the Indians had ceased for a time, as I looked out on a reach of prairie, at about the distance of a mile away, some men emerged from the hillsides. They seemed to be advancing in a line, and in regular order. Then I heard what seemed to be a far-off singing. They were singing a dirge. The sound came nearer and nearer, and the singers showed more and more plainly. There was something peculiar about their appearance. They came half walking, half running, up the slope toward our house, singing the dirge as they came. Each of them was dragging an unstripped willow-branch, which trailed on the ground.

"When they came close enough to be recognized, I saw the blood streaming from the left arm of each of them. The broken end of the willow-branch was thrust through the thick flesh of the upper-arm of each one, while the tops and the boughs, leaves and all, trailed on the ground. They had walked the distance of a mile, singing the death-dirge, in honor of my dead brother.

"The impression it made on me is almost as vivid today as it was then—this remembrance of my brother's death. I think it will please my mother to know that the memory of him still lives, and she will like to know that the baby's sketch, which accompanies this article, has been published. It is a hasty sketch, taken of Louis when he was a baby, by some wandering artist, at the time of the Mormon emigration to Utah. She says she was standing, with Louis in her arms, by the Missouri river, when the artist got off the steamboat, while it was unloading its passengers, and that he made the sketch, took the leaf out of the book, and handed it to her as he stood on the gang-plank, while the whistle sounded."

The Captive's Song

M any years ago, before the Omaha Indians sold to the government the land on which Omaha now stands, I heard an Indian captive sing a song which I can never forget.

We were living then at Bellevue, although the rest of the Omahas were living in mud lodges over seventy-eight miles up the river, where Homer now stands, and a few that were scattered along the banks of the river between Homer and Bellevue. There was not even a single house where Omaha now stands.

The Pawnees were on the war-path, and knowing the Spaniards had many horses, they had gone far west and made a raid, bringing home many horses and five young Spanish boys as captives, whom they had found herding horses.

They brought the captives home without any trouble, for the Spaniards did not know of their loss for some time, as the herds were a long way from their homes, and the herders had provisions with them. There were no English people here at all then—only Frenchmen, mostly traders. Some of them came up here from St. Louis, and told our agent that the Pawnees had five Spanish captives. Our agent went down, and the Pawnees gave up the captives to him, and he brought them back with him to the Omahas. While waiting for the Omahas to come down to Bellevue, they stayed at our house, and I saw the captives. There were two about sixteen or eighteen years old, one about ten, and the youngest eight years old. The youngest one held on to the coat of the agent, for he was afraid of the new Indian tribe.

Just before the Spanish captives arrived at Bellevue, an event occurred among the Indians who were camped along the river.

An Indian named Nettle (Sha-nug-a-hi) had built a straw hut among the bluffs, close to the river, and in this abandoned hut a Frenchman, coming from the Sioux country, had taken refuge. It seems his feet had been frozen, and unable to walk farther, he was resting in the hut when found by an Omaha Indian, who had been hunting deer.

Why he committed the crime we do not know, but he shot the poor Frenchman. He then told every Indian hunter whom he met he had killed a white man, because No Heart, an Omaha Indian, had been killed by an Iowa Indian. Happening to meet his brother, who was also out hunting, he took him back to the straw hut to see the white man he had killed. Wa-o-ga, the brother, seeing the Frenchman was still alive, and suffering, although mortally wounded, said that out of pity he put an end to his sufferings.

Big Elk was then our head chief. He was a very good man, and one of the greatest chiefs the Omahas ever had. He was well known by the French and Spaniards, and respected by both white people and Indians.

It was before I was married to Iron Eye, and he and his father had just returned from hunting, near Homer, when the old chief came into the tent and whispered a few words to your grandfather. Your father knew it must be something important that Big Elk was telling. So when the old chief had gone, he asked him what it was.

"He has sent the following message to the authorities at St. Louis," your grandfather said, "which he wishes me to deliver. Wa-o-ga's brother has killed a white man, and he is afraid not only that the white men may become incensed at the tribe, but that the Omahas may be tempted to repeat the crime some day, and Big Elk wishes the authorities to take the crime in hand and punish the offender, as an example for the rest."

As our agent was then at Bellevue, your father and grandfather came down to Bellevue, on their way to St. Louis, and gave the message sent by the head chief.

The agent sent Village Maker up after the murderer, and he was brought down to Bellevue with Big Elk and Wa-nun-sun-da.

The captive was guarded, but on the second day he made his escape. They followed him up to the mud lodge village at Homer, and watched for him and searched his tent, but they did not find him, and it was only after close watching that near midnight they caught him as he was stealing into his tent.

Village Maker and Chief Big Elk again brought him down to Bellevue, and he was going to be taken down to St. Louis with the Spanish captives, who were to be returned to their Spanish friends. This time the murderer's brother, Wa-o-ga, was also to be taken down.

Two boats, hollowed out of great cottonwood logs, were laid along side of each other, and fastened together by nailing boards across, and thus forming a platform on which the passengers were to sit. There were to be fourteen passengers, besides bedding and provisions, for it was a long trip in those days from Bellevue to St. Louis.

It was a beautiful day in early spring that the captives were to be taken down, the Spaniards to find freedom, the Indians to find captivity.

Our house was two stories high, and had a balcony, and I stood looking down at the beautiful green yard below, when I saw the Indian captive come out of the employes' quarters. He was dressed in buckskin leggins and buffalo robe, and his long, black hair hung down below his shoulders. He took his place in the middle of the green yard, and cast a long, searching look around, with perfect despair on his face. He seemed to realize the hopelessness of his captivity. His wild, free life was over; what mattered else? Then he sang his song:

Un winwata bltha dan,
Gunata ha hata dan?
Un winwata bltha dan,
Gunata hata dan?
Inshaga wanunkcha shanun;
Winwata bltha dan
Gunatun hata dan?
(Where can I go
That I might live forever?
Where can I go
That I might live forever?
The old fathers have gone to the spirit-land,
Where can I go
That we might live together?)

The song thrilled me through and through, and I thought, how true it is, for he meant that wherever we go, we will always have death before us—we cannot avoid it—that no matter what he did nor where he went, he could not live forever, that all his forefathers had gone to the spirit land, and how could he expect to escape death. When he finished his song he returned to the quarters from whence he had come. There was perfect silence, and no one spoke; they only felt that he had sung the truth.

They started down the river: Big Elk, the agent, your father and your grandfather, the two Indian captives, the young Spaniards, Village Maker, Wa-nun-sun-da and Joe Roubridaux, all in the boat I told you about. They were only a few days' travel from St. Louis, when a storm came up. As long as they kept close to the bank they were safe, but the agent ordered them to cross the river, in hopes of finding a steam-boat landing. They could see the big white-capped waves, and the water was so much rougher near the middle of the river.

Your father said, "No, the boat will sink if we cross; keep where you are." But the agent insisting, the rash attempt was made. When they were in the middle of the river, the boat began to sink, and the agent was the first to jump into the water and swim for the shore. How he ever had the strength to reach it, they did not know, for he had on a heavy fur coat and heavy boots. Big Elk, Wa-nun-sun-da and Village Maker also struck out for the shore, and safely reached it, as well as Joe Roubrideaux.

Your father told the young Spaniards to cling to the boat, but the three older ones struck out for the shore, and soon sank. The two little ones obeyed, and he heard them both praying as they clung to the boat. Through all their captivity, the little Spaniards never forgot to say their prayers, and every night knelt down, and now, in time of great peril, they turned to God for help, and He heard them, for they were both saved, and later returned to their Spanish friends.

Imitating the cry of a bear, the Indian captive, when he saw the others jump from the boat, made one great effort and broke his handcuffs. With his free hands he took the heavy log chain that bound his feet together and threw it over his shoulder, ready to jump into the water.

"The iron will make you sink," your father shouted, but the captive jumped. As he was sinking, your father, with one hand, grasped him by the hair, and pulled him up onto the platform. Perhaps the captive remembered his song; anyway, he made one long jump, and sank straight down, never to rise again.

Wa-o-ga, clinging to the boat, was also saved.

Your father and grandfather stayed in the boat, and drifted safely to land with the two Spanish boys. The others who had swum ashore had run along the bank, keeping the boat in sight.

Just then a steamboat, on its way to the Yellowstone, made a timely appearance, for the party had lost provisions and bedding, and those who had swum ashore were cold. The agent told them of their predicament, and without stopping, the men on the steamboat threw them a ham, a box of crackers, clothing and blankets. They would have had a hard time reaching St. Louis otherwise, for at that time there were no settlements, and not a house between Bellevue and St. Louis, except a few log huts where St. Joe now is.

On reaching St. Louis, Wa-o-ga was put in jail for three days. He was put under guard, and the Omahas told to furnish him with dry bread and water. Your father pitied him, and would take a loaf of bread, and hollowing one end, would put in a piece of meat and close it up again. At the end of the three days Wa-o-ga was led out to his trial.

It was long before the day when Judge Dundy, of Omaha, rendered his famous decision that "an Indian is a man," and had the same privilege a white man had in a court of law. In those days, an Indian could be taken up for any crime, but. he could not have any white man punished in a court of law, no matter what crime the white man had committed against an Indian. Since Judge Dundy's decision, we have found, as one of our own race has said, "Law is liberty."

Wa-o-ga's anxiety was ended, and he was a free man, for he told the authorities that out of mercy for the poor man's suffering he had ended his life, after his brother had mortally wounded him.

The party had to walk home from St. Louis, but they brought many things home, which they had carried all that distance.

Indian Picture Writing

 Buffalo very plenty.

 Buffalo very plenty.

 Many horses die of starvation.

 Great abundance of buffalo meat.

 White soldiers make their first appearance in the country.

 A French-Canadian built a trading store of dry timber.

 The comet appeared.

 The stars fell.

 An eclipse of the sun.

Indian Folk Lore Story

There was an old woman who lived all alone, the Rabbit was her son and the old woman was Mother Earth. Rabbit had a magic skin, by which he exercised all his powers. It was a rabbit skin, the perfect image of himself. Rabbit lived with the old woman, and brought her game. The old woman was the mother of all living creatures, feeding them on things which grew up out of herself. Grandmother Mazhun* said to her grandson, 'All the people are my children, all the men are your fathers, all the women your mothers, and all the children your uncles and aunts.'

"And God made a man and put him on the earth to take care of the people, but the man God sent hated the people, and looked on them as his property. This man took all the buffalo and deer and put them in herds, and made the people take care of them, but did not allow them to kill any to eat, so the people were nearly starved.

"Grandmother Mazhun said to Rabbit: 'I thought I told you to be kind to your fathers and mothers.'

"That was all she said, and spoke no more.

"'I will see about this, said Rabbit.'

"Then Rabbit went on a journey to see this man, and took his magic skin with him. He said nothing to Grandmother Mazhun about his project. As he was going along, he passed a handsome man.

"'I have been waiting a long time,' said the man. 'You have been slow in coming.'

"'I hurried,' replied Rabbit, 'but I was slow, after all,' and in an instant he was transformed into a handsome young man, himself.

"This splendid young brave whom Rabbit met was Umba.† They traveled on together, and soon overtook another handsome man. He had a war club and a tobacco bag. This was Ka.‡

"'I have been waiting a long time,' said he, 'and you did not come.'

"The three walked on together, until they came to where the herders were taking care of the buffalo and deer. A little fawn had been neglected

---

* Mazhun—The Earth.
† Umba—Light of the Sun.
‡ Ka—Turtle.

by the herders, or escaped by accident, and Rabbit said, 'I will take this fawn with me.'

"The fawn followed, and the four went on until they came to the place where the man was whom God had placed on the earth to take care of the people.

"'You have come to challenge me, have you?' said he to Rabbit. 'What have you brought Ka along with you for? He is always inventing tricks and devices to deceive.'

"'I have come to challenge you,' said Rabbit. 'Let us fix upon the wager. What will you bet?'

"'I will throw all the people over whom I rule,' said the man, 'for that seems to be what you want. If you win, you shall have them.'

"Then they sat down to gamble with reeds.* Rabbit won every time. He won the buffalo, and turned them out of the herds to roam at will. He won the deer and elk, and all the people, and told them to go where they pleased.

"At last the man said, 'Let us try something else besides these reeds.'

"'What do you want to try now?' asked Rabbit.

"'We will wager on walking in the same tracks,' said the man.

"'All right,' said Rabbit.

"'What animal will you use?' asked the man.

"'My little fawn,' said Rabbit. 'And what animal will you use?'

"'The wild cat,' he replied.

"There was a clump of wild goosberry bushes near by. It was agreed that around it the track should be made. Rabbit caused a snow to fall, and the trial began.

"The fawn made his own trail, and the wild cat his, and they went around and around in their circles for a long time.

"Ka got out of patience, and whispered to Umba, 'That's enough.'

"'Wah! let us do everything fair,' said Umba.

"Ka wanted to win by a trick, but Umba would not listen to him. Finally, after the thing had gone on for a long time, each animal always stepping exactly in the former tracks, Ka lost his patience altogether, and said:

"'Come, make an end of this.'

---

* The game is played by throwing a bundle of reeds, something over a foot long, on the ground, and then grasping as many as possible in the hands at once. He who grasps an even number wins.

"The man who was sitting near by gave a little puff, Ka caught the puff and turned it into a great hurricane. The wild cat fell over and put his foot out of the track.

"'You did that,' said the man to Ka, and he struck Ka on the head. The blow mashed all the bones, and the brains all ran out.

"That is the reason the turtle's head is full of little bones and no brains.

"At the conclusion of this game, Rabbit turned loose the bears and all the animals with fur, and gave the man the name of 'Cinidawagithe'.*

"Rabbit thought he would go through the country a little and see how the people liked all this, so he took up his magic skin, and said to Ka, 'You watch Cinidawagithe while I am gone.' As Rabbit took up the skin, it was so transformed that it looked exactly like him, so he put it down and left it there.

"Rabbit noticed that Cinidawagithe did not have his soul with him,† and he said: 'If we kill him, his soul will not be dead, but will take some other form, and live on.'

"Rabbit then went to the place where Cinidawagithe's wife was, to inquire of her where he had hidden his soul.

"The magic skin was there in the place where the contest was made, and Cinidawagithe, not knowing Rabbit was gone, said to Ka: 'We will play another game.'

"'What?' asked Ka.

"'We will see who can keep his eyes open the longest without winking.'

"'I will have the eagle play for me,' said Cinidawagithe.

"'Rabbit will play on our side,' said Ka.

"Then he put two acorns in the place for eyes in the magic skin, and the eagle sat down by the side of it, with eyes wide open, to make the trial, while he and Umba sat watching.

"Meanwhile, Rabbit went to Cinidwagithe's wife's tent, having on the way transformed himself to look exactly like her husband.

"'I have come, wife,' he said, 'to rest awhile.'

"'No, no, Rabbit,' she replied, I know you.'

"'I am myself, and I have come to rest; give me some dinner.'

---

* Muskrat.
† A belief of universal acceptance among Indians is that it is possible for the body to live without the soul.

"Finally the woman was persuaded to believe Rabbit was her husband, and gave him his dinner and supper; but being in such fear of her husband, she again insisted in great earnestness that he was Rabbit.

"'Yes, it is I,' said Rabbit. 'Your husband is very bad; if he knew I staid here, he would kill you. If you keep still I will save you alive. Now tell me, where did your husband hide his soul?'

"'There is a very large lake,' said the woman, 'by it there is a loon, and this loon has my husband's soul in charge.'

"The woman was very much afraid of both Cinidawagithe and Rabbit, so she insisted that the Rabbit must use all his power and exercise all his strategy to kill the loon.

"'You can only kill it,' she said, 'by taking out its heart. No one has been able to get near it.'

"Rabbit started out to hunt the loon. He soon came across an old beaver woman.

"'I have been hunting,' he said to her.

"'What are you hunting?' she asked.

"'I want to know of you something.'

"'What have I got that you want?' she asked, somewhat surprised.

"'If you will lend me what I want,' Rabbit replied, 'I will pay you well.'

"'Well, tell me what it is that you want,' she said.

"Rabbit, without further ado, said plainly: 'I want your heart, lend it to me.'

"The beaver woman took out her heart and gave it to Rabbit, and Rabbit said:

"'To pay you for this I will give you a tomahawk to cut down trees with, and the work you do with it shall be better than man can do.' And he gave her her teeth.

"This is how beavers get their sharp teeth.

"All this time Cinidawagithe did not know that Rabbit had gone. He thought the magic skin was the real Rabbit.

"After awhile Rabbit came near the lake, and called the loon. It answered.

"'Rabbit, I know you,' said the loon, and then went further away.

"Rabbit called it again and again, and at last said:

"'It is I; I have come to see how my soul is getting along.'

"The loon was finally deceived and gave Rabbit the soul of Cinidawagithe. He kept it, and then gave back to the loon the heart the Beaver woman had given him.

"'This does not look like the same thing I gave you,' said the loon.

"Rabbit assured the loon that it was, and then went straight to Cinidawagithe's wife.

"'I have accomplished it,' he said. 'It was a hard task, but I succeeded.'

"Then he sat down right in front of her and cut the soul into small pieces.

"'Now,' said he, 'You are safe. If Cinidawagithe tries to kill you, he can't.'

"Rabbit went back where Umba, Ka and Cinidawagithe were making the trial between the eagle and the magic skin with acorns for eyes, and there the eagle sat, gazing, not having winked even once.

"Ka had gotten entirely out of patience again, and as Rabbit came up, said to Umba:

"'Let us finish this; I am tired of it.'

"'Let us wait,' Umba quietly replied. 'This is the last trial; we have nearly finished all we came to do.'

"But Ka wouldn't wait any longer; his patience was all gone, and he replied:

"'Let us end it.'

"'All right,' said Umba, and blew a breath in Ka's mouth, Ka blew it out again, and then fell a great rain. The water ran down in the eagle's eyes and made him wink.

"Ka jumped up and shouted:

"'We have won! We have won! Wa, we have won!'

"This made Cinidawagithe very angry, and he pounded Ka's head until it was flat.

"That is how the turtles came to have flat heads.

"Then Rabbit spoke in his proper person to Cinidawagithe, and said:

"'Wakanda* put you here to take care of the people, but you had a bad heart, and were selfish. I might kill you, but I will turn you into a muskrat. You shall have no soul, and must always live among the fishes.'"

---

* God—Sacred One.

OMAHA IN 1898

Omaha city, the metropolis of Nebraska, is situated midway between the oceans, and is the center of the greatest agricultural region on the globe. After the purchase of the land from the Indians, Omaha has gradually grown from the Indian wigwams of 1854 to the now populous city of 154,000 inhabitants. Her churches and schools are among the finest and best. Her manufacturing and jobbing houses, smelting and refining works, linseed oil mills and white lead works all have an extensive trade.

Omaha is one of the greatest live stock markets in the world, and that accounts for her immense packing houses. This, and the enormous amount of agricultural productions in the surrounding fertile country, has made for her a great railroad center, her systems of transportation reaching far into the British territory on the north, to the Gulf of Mexico on the south, to the Atlantic Ocean on the east, and the Pacific on the west. Only those who visit the city can judge correctly concerning what faithful and energetic citizens can accomplish in a few short years. It is probably true to say that on no spot on the face of the whole earth could such advancement be shown in the last fifty years. Then a wilderness inhabited only by native tribes, now a city in the front rank of modern civilization.

Not only on its commercial side has Omaha prospered. While its citizens have sought after wealth with the eagerness that everywhere characterizes the American citizen, they have not forgotten the far more real, though immaterial things, which lie at the foundation of all human progress and all real happiness. Very many persons have risen to distinction in literature, whose first attempts were made in Omaha. The votaries of art, for art's sake, can be found all over these plains, while in Omaha there is an art gallery not equalled in any city of the same size in the United States. Several successful novels have been written, and the scenes laid in this city. Some writers of humor, whose reputations are now as wide as the nation, and one who gained a world-wide audience, first attracted attention through work done on Nebraska publications.

Nebraska

The citizenship of Nebraska is noted for its quick adaptation to the needs of every occasion as it arises. Whether it is famine or war, drouth or flood, the men of Nebraska know what to do, and do it without hesitation. When the call was made for food for the starving women and children of Cuba, a Nebraska newspaper collected and forwarded a whole train load of supplies within ten days. The state was one of the first to furnish its full quota of troops, and has ever since been begging the government to allow it to send more than its quota. A newspaper man, as part of his daily work, on the day the call for troops was made, wrote and printed the two poems reproduced in this booklet, descriptive of a Cuban mother and child and the landing of our troops on Cuban soil.

The Cuban Mother

"Mother, why look all day at the sea?
Come to the hut and sit thou with me.
Hunger has gone and all of the pain,
Come, mother, come, you look but in vain"

"Not so, my child, not so,
A faint, dark line I see,
'Tis dim, and dull and low,
Far out upon the sea.
Oh! God, Oh! can it be
The ships from northern lands,
With food for you, for me?
Gathered with loving hands—
Oh! can it be, can it be?"

"Mother, why look all day at the sea?
Come to the hut and sit thou by me,
No one is here since baby has died.
Come to the hut and sit by my side."

"Be brave, my child, be brave,
The ships I plainly see.
They come! they come to save!
With food for you, for me.
The northern mother told
Of baby's dying cry.
I see the flag unfold
And gleam against the sky."

"Mother, why look all day at the sea?
Come to the hut and sit thou with me.
May I not lay my head on your knee?
Mother, you dream, there's naught on the sea."

"I dream not. Now I see
The red, the white, the blue—

SUSETTE LA FLESCHE AND FANNIE REED GRIFFIN

> *The flag of liberty.*
> *They come! they come! It's true,*
> *Be brave, my child, be brave,*
> *They heard the children's cry,*
> *They come, they come to save,*
> *Praise be to God on high."*

While the citizenship of the state is made up of various nationalities, including English, Germans, Swedes, Norwegians, Poles, Frenchmen, Russians, Swiss, Austrians, Bohemians, Cubans, Spaniards, Indians, Armenians, Greeks and Negroes, we all live in peace together, and there are no race problems to trouble society. At the same time, the United States census shows that Nebraska has less illiteracy than any other state in the Union. It has statesmen and scientists whose names are household words in every civilized land.

Its great university, located at Lincoln, open and free to all, gives a liberal education to 2,000 students every year. Four tribes of Indians are permanently located in the state, and all of them are making commendable progress in the arts of civilization. Fifty years ago Nebraska was a trackless wilderness. Today it is dotted with cities, grid-ironed with railroads, and filled with schools, churches and higher institutions of learning. Men of every race and of every country have found a home here, where we live in peace, and if one suffers, it is the concern of all.

Our Boys in Cuba

Well, Cuban mothers, they have come,
    That is, what's left of them,
Through fire and smoke and bursting bomb,
    'Cross fields of blood, by dying men,
Where bullets rained, and the fierce scream
    Of shell—a bloody track.
Now drink, drink from my canteen,
    Eat from my haversack.

What? Don't hesitate. It's for you.
    (How pale she is and wan,
And that strange talk to me is new,
    The language of the Don.
How ill she is, and thin and lean.
    Those eyes! How large and black)
Don't weep! Drink from my canteen,
    Eat from my haversack.

What? (The voice is strange and low,
    A wailing, full of fears,
But there's one language all men know,
    It speaks through woman's tears.)
You heard our shou's and saw the gleam
    Of bayonets. The Dons ran back.
We've come. Drink from my canteen,
    Eat from my haversack.

"Senor." Oh, don't call me senor,
    I'm but a farmer lad,
Who left his plow to go to war.
    We just got fighting mad
'Bout starving women, children's screams
    And Weyler's bloody track.
So drink, drink from our canteens,
    Eat from the haversack.

A Note About the Authors

Susette La Flesche (1854–1903) was a Native American writer, lecturer, and illustrator. Born to a family of Ponca, Iowa, French, and English ancestry, La Flesche, the daughter of Omaha Chief Joseph La Flesche, was given the name Inshata Theumba, or "Bright Eyes." Raised on the Omaha Reservation, she was sent to a girls' school in Elizabeth, New Jersey, where she developed a talent for writing and drawing. She returned to the home upon graduating to serve as the first American-educated teacher on the Omaha Reservation, where she soon gained a reputation as a political activist and loyal interpreter for Chief Standing Bear. She married abolitionist newspaperman Thomas Tibbles in 1881, and together they toured the country to report on the conditions experienced by Native Americans in a time of genocide and government oppression. She eventually settled on the Omaha Reservation, where she spent the remainder of her life.

Fannie Reed Griffin was a biographer and folklorist.

A Note from the Publisher

Spanning many genres, from non-fiction essays to literature classics to children's books and lyric poetry, Mint Edition books showcase the master works of our time in a modern new package. The text is freshly typeset, is clean and easy to read, and features a new note about the author in each volume. Many books also include exclusive new introductory material. Every book boasts a striking new cover, which makes it as appropriate for collecting as it is for gift giving. Mint Edition books are only printed when a reader orders them, so natural resources are not wasted. We're proud that our books are never manufactured in excess and exist only in the exact quantity they need to be read and enjoyed.

Discover more of your favorite classics with Bookfinity™.

- Track your reading with custom book lists.
- Get great book recommendations for your personalized Reader Type.
- Add reviews for your favorite books.
- AND MUCH MORE!

Visit **bookfinity.com** and take the fun Reader Type quiz to get started.

Enjoy our classic and modern companion pairings!